POOL OF PERIL
AND THE

DEAR READER,

When I was around eight years old, I took a trip to France with my cousins and my uncle and aunty. We went to the beach. The first thing I wanted to do when I got there was go to the water, so I did. We clung onto this big flatable and drifted out into the sea; everything was totally fine until I realized that I couldn't touch the ground with my feet. **THE PANIC** hit me, my heart began to beat so fast, and all I wanted to do was to get out of the water.

Nothing bad happened to me, but since then, one thing I've always feared is being in water so deep that my feet can't touch the ground. Swimming was completely out of the question, and for almost twenty years of my life, it stayed like that.

My partner, Martha, loved swimming, though. It was one of her favourite things to do, so, of course, she wanted to share that with me. She kept asking if I wanted to learn to swim. I'd always say yes but never planned to do it. Until one day, I decided to be brave and go.

I booked a swimming lesson. I was planning to only go once, to get Martha off my back. But when I went, I realized that I really liked swimming. I didn't want

Grandad patted Marvin on the shoulder.

'I think it's time we moved forward,' he said with a smile.

'Oh, sorry,' Marvin said. He glanced ahead. A space had opened up in the queue. The entrance to the brand new water park, Wave World, was only a couple of steps away now.

Entrance

'So, little one, are you excited?' Grandad said.

'Yeah, of course I am,' Marvin replied in a very quiet voice. He wasn't lying, part of him *was* excited. It was his best friend's birthday and Joe's birthday was always fun! It's just that having it here, at Wave World, made Marvin feel uneasy. It wasn't that Marvin didn't like the water (he could see Joe and his family now, and couldn't wait to join them) but at the same time, he didn't want to run into **THE PANIC** again.

THE PANIC made his heart suddenly thud in his chest. **THE PANIC** made him forget his swimming lessons. **THE PANIC** made him want to get out of the pool.

'It's okay to feel nervous or to be scared,' Grandad said.

A high pitched beeping came from Marvin's backpack, then a small round robot head poked out of the top. It was Pixel, Marvin's robot sidekick.

Marvin had a super-suit that transformed him into a superhero called Marv. He took the suit and Pixel everywhere with him, 'just in case', as his grandad would say. Today he felt like he needed them with him more than ever.

'Grandad, were you ever a little nervous when you were in the water?' Marvin asked. Grandad reached into his pocket and pulled out his wallet. In it was a newspaper clipping.

TALENTED DIVER BEATS RECORD FOR HIGHEST DIVE

A boy who looked like a younger version of Grandad was photographed standing on the edge of a diving board, over a pool of water. 'So, you weren't nervous around water,' Marvin said, shoulders slumped.

Grandad pulled down his sunglasses and winked.

'Let me tell you the story. At our local swimming pool, they built this brand new diving board. 'And so, to promote it to the community they asked me, their local superhero, to show everyone that it was safe and fun. I've always been a good swimmer but I was terrified of diving. Still, I said yes—'

'And tried not to think about it until

it snuck up on you?' Marvin interrupted, thinking about what he had done when Joe had invited him to Wave World.

'Well, yes, I did do exactly that,' Grandad said with a sheepish smile. 'But, I ended up completing the dive.'

'So, you just beat your fear, just like that?' Marvin leaned forward and said.

'I wish! I had to train that whole week with a friend before I even felt comfortable getting on that huge diving board. But still, on the day of the dive my stomach was in a complete state, it was flipping all over the shop. I kept pushing back the time for my dive and ended up delaying so much that the news crew almost left.' Grandad and Marvin burst into laughter.

'But how did you do it? How did you beat your fear?'

Grandad chuckled and scratched his beard. 'I realized that *sometimes you just have to jump*. I knew that I really wanted to do that dive, and the only thing holding me back was my fear. Eventually, I found my courage and did it,' Grandad said.

Marvin gazed up at his Grandad and smiled.

'Tickets please,' said the man in the entrance booth.

They were now at the front of the queue. Grandad handed over their tickets and they walked through the gates. As soon as they got in, Joe came bounding towards them.

'Happy Birthday, Joe!' Grandad said. 'Where are your parents? I'll go say hello.' Joe pointed behind him and Grandad moved off in that direction.

'You're finally here! This water park is so huge. It has everything. We're going to have so much fun today!' Joe said.

'Yeah, erm, I can't wait,' Marvin said, crossing his arms over his chest and glancing around. The place was packed. 'There are so many people here.'

'Yeah, the queues for all the rides are super long.' Joe sighed. 'We'll still have a ton of fun, but you know I kinda wish we had the whole place to ourselves. Imagine what that would be like!'

Marvin didn't really want to imagine anything about the water park right now.

'Come on, you need to get changed, then we can go jump in the pool!' Joe continued.

'That sounds so . . .' Marvin hesitated, staring at one of the pools. It looked so deep. Did it even *have* a bottom? ' . . . fun,' Marvin squeezed the word out of his mouth.

Joe pulled Marvin through Wave World, all the way to the changing rooms. Marvin went inside and gave a great big sigh of relief. It was good to get away from those pesky pools for a moment.

Pixel jumped out of his backpack waving Marvin's swimming shorts.

'I've been monitoring the pool water and there seems to be a problem here,' she said.

'Are you sure it's okay for you to come out of the bag?' he whispered. 'I think you should stay in my bag today, Pixel. I don't want to risk you falling in the water and rusting!'

'I don't think I'm capable of rusting,' Pixel said slowly. She sounded unsure.

'Do you really want to risk it?' Marvin bent down and rubbed Pixels head.

'To continue, the pool water has a 99% chance of—' Pixel started, but she didn't get to finish. Marvin scooped her up and plopped her down into his bag again.

'I know, I know. You're probably nervous about the pools, just like me, right? But like Grandad said, we just need to find the courage to face our fears.'

CHAPTER 2

'Come on Marvin. The big pool is just over there!' Joe pointed, hopping with excitement. Marvin looked over at a ginormous pool filled with so much water and so many people.

'Yes. I can see it,' Marvin said with a nervous swallow. He wished so much that he could find the courage that his grandad had talked about, but right now he just couldn't find it. Marvin paused, thinking as hard as he could and he had an idea. 'Let's definitely do it, but first I just need to get a drink.'

'A drink?' Joe's eyebrows raised.

'Yes, everyone knows that you can't swim properly if you're thirsty. Grandad gave me some coins, come on, let's find a vending machine!'

Marvin and Joe went off through Wave World searching for a vending machine, and it didn't take long for them to find one.

'Are you ready for the pool now?' Joe asked as Marvin sipped his water.

Marvin reached back and scratched his head, trying his best to smile.

'Almost. After drinking all that water I just need to go to the toilet. I'll only be a minute,' Marvin said.

Marvin and Joe set off again, this time looking for the toilets. They got there pretty quickly, and to Marvin's dismay, there wasn't a queue. Joe waited outside and as soon as Marvin was out Joe asked him again.

'So, are you ready for the big pool now?' Joe said.

'I'm totally ready. I can't wait to go.' Marvin glanced around looking for something, anything that would give him an excuse not to get in that big pool. 'It looks like your little brother is lonely in the baby pool. Maybe we should join him,' Marvin shrugged. 'If you want.'

Joe frowned. 'My parents are with him. He'll be fine.'

'Are you sure? There's nothing wrong with checking on your brother,' Marvin said. Joe's frown grew. Marvin knew that it was the end of the road. Joe was getting impatient. 'We don't need to check. Let's go over to the big pool,' Marvin said, hoping courage would finally find him there.'

'I just need to go leave my bag with my grandad,' Marvin said, glad to have another excuse to delay getting in the water a little longer. He slowly walked over to Grandad, who was sat by the side of the pool reading a book. 'Just leaving my bag here.'

Grandad lowered his sunglasses and gave Marvin a wink.

'Come on Marvin!' Joe cried. He ran into the pool, splashing water all around him.

Marvin crept over to the pool and dipped a toe in. The water was warm. He slid a foot into the pool.

'That wasn't so bad,' Marvin said to himself.

He kept on going, one foot after the other and soon the water was all the

way up to his knees. Marvin looked up with a grin on his face, but Joe was nowhere to be found. The pool was full of people and Joe was somewhere amongst the crowd. Marvin just had to find him.

'Joe!' Marvin cried out, wading forward. 'Joe!' He shouted again, but no one responded. Where was Joe? Marvin looked down, the water was up to his waist now. **THE PANIC** struck. It wobbled up his legs, all the way to his chest. Marvin

turned and began to scurry back to more shallow water, but before he could reach it he heard somebody scream.

'SHARK!'

Marvin's head whipped around.

'THERE'S A SHARK IN THE WATER!' someone bellowed.

All at once, people began to run.
THE PANIC wasn't just with Marvin,
now it was in everybody. There was a
stampede towards the pool edge.

A lifeguard scrambled off his chair and blew his whistle.

'Order! Order in the pool!' Everyone stopped for a moment. The lifeguard peered into the water then yelled at the top of his lungs. 'Actually, there are three sharks! Run!'

THE PANIC wanted Marvin to turn and run too. 'Water was bad enough and now there were sharks! But he didn't run. Deep down Marvin had this other feeling. He didn't know what it was but it kept him standing still as people barged past him. He had to find Joe and make sure he was okay.'

A shadow slithered just under the surface of the water, then a shark fin slowly slid up from beneath the waves.

Marvin gasped. There really were sharks in the pool!

'Marvin, come on. No time for dallying around,' Grandad called out, wading out into the pool.

'Joe!' Marvin cried as he searched for his friend. 'Marvin!' Grandad called out again.

Marvin knew he couldn't leave Joe behind—he needed to come up with a plan and fast.

Marvin followed his grandad out of the pool.

'Come on,' said Grandad. 'Let's grab your swimming bag and go.' The lifeguard led them away from the pool. There, Marvin found Joe.

'Joe!' Marvin cried out when he saw him. Marvin and his Grandad huddled over by Joe and his family. 'I thought I lost you,' he said wrapping, his arms around Joe.

'Don't worry everyone! We're going to sort this out!' one of the lifeguards addressed the grumbling crowd.

'Really you're going to "sort out" sharks?' Somebody called out from the crowd. 'How're you going to do that?!'

'Well, we don't know yet,' the lifeguard said, scratching his head. 'We've never had sharks in the pool before.' The crowd

erupted into chatter again.

'Sharks. That's terrifying,' Joe's father, a man with a very bushy moustache, said. 'Where did they come from? We're in a pool, not the sea.' His teeth were chattering, and he wasn't the only one. A cool breeze wooshed past. Marvin wrapped his arms around himself. They were all wet and miserable.

'W-what are we going to do?' Joe said.

What *were* they going to do? Marvin thought to himself.

CHAPTER 3

Were the sharks still there? Marvin decided to check. He walked up to Wave World entrance and peered inside.

Three shark fins swirled around the big pool, going round and round in a circle. Marvin tried to keep an eye on them, but something kept getting in the way. It moved back and forth across the surface of the pool.

Suddenly, whatever it was burst up into the air and landed at the side of the pool. It was a person, a girl! She wore a super-suit that looked like it was built for the pool. It had webbed fingers and toes. On her head was a tight swimming cap. The whole super suit was rubbery and black. On her face was a massive grin.

Marvin held his breath. He knew what she looked like. A **supervillain**!

She walked over to the tannoy at the lifeguard's seat, cleared her throat, picked up the microphone and began to speak,

'Here's an announcement for you losers! I am Hydro the supervillain, and this is now MY water park!' Hydro's voice boomed out of the speakers. 'That's right! You heard me! It's all mine! And if any of you disagree with me then you have a little conversation with my SHARKS!' She finished with a flourish, slamming the microphone down.

The crowd outside fell into a stunned silence. They walked over to where Marvin was and looked in at Hydro.

Hydro pranced around the water park doing whatever she wanted. And what she wanted to do was everything you're not supposed to do at a pool. She went over to the ice cream stall and helped herself to tons of ice cream without paying. She ran between the pools at super speed, without getting told off by the lifeguards. And, she dive-bombed into the pools from all angles, splashing water everywhere. And when she was done with all that she filled the pools with huge inflatable. There were giant hotdogs, pizza slices, doughnuts, unicorns, flamingos, crocodiles, anything you could think of, Hydro had an

inflatable version. Finally, a giant black
inflatable castle appeared floating in
the middle of the largest pool where Joe
and Marvin had been only moments
before.

Marvin heard a deep sigh behind
him. He turned around to see Joe looking
miserable, with his head down. Marvin
could see tears starting to peek out of the

corner of Joe's eyes. Marvin felt heavy in his chest. He understood why Joe was upset. Hydro had ruined his entire birthday party, and you only got one of those a year!

Marvin knew he couldn't let Hydro ruin Joe and everyone else's day, but still a tiny part of him felt a little bit relieved that Hydro had arrived. After all, it meant that he didn't have to spend any more time in the pool.

A high pitched beeping suddenly erupted from Marvin's swimming bag. Pixel!

'Back in a minute,' Marvin said to Grandad.

Marvin walked away from the crowd until he was out of sight, then he opened up his swimming bag.

'SUPERVILLAIN DETECTED!

SUPERVILLAIN DETECTED!'

Pixel said as she popped out of the bag.

'You're right, but you're a little late,' Marvin said.

'Is that correct? Sorry, I was busy carrying out internal scans to make sure my anti-rust feature was active.'

'Yep, she's been out causing mayhem for a while now.' Marvin pointed back at the water park.

Pixel cocked her head to one side. 'Not
surprising. The pool water did indicate
that there was a 99% chance of sharks.
Sharks always come with supervillains.'

'You know, maybe we don't have to save the day this time. It might be good to let someone else take care of things.'. Marvin's shoulders were hunched and he stared at the ground.

'But you're a superhero and I'm a sidekick! I've carried out searches in the area and I can't find any other superheroes. Especially no superheroes whose best friend's birthday is currently being ruined by a supervillain.' Pixel frowned, it was the first time Marvin had seen her do that.

'I guess we are the only ones who can help,' Marvin groaned.

'Then why aren't you in your super-suit stopping her?' Pixel said.

Marvin knew the reason but he didn't want to say. There was that tiny part of him that didn't want to be in the pool. It was **THE PANIC**. Now it was keeping him from helping people. Marvin took a deep breath, looked at Pixel and then smiled despite his fear, despite **THE PANIC**.

'I'm ready,' Marvin said 'Let's go be heroes!'

Pixel beeped loudly and spun around in circles. Marvin ducked behind a tree and threw on his super-suit.

Marvin was now **MARV**!

Together they headed back towards Wave World entrance.

Whispers came from the crowd outside as Marv got close.

'Is that a superhero?!' Someone said.

'Not just any superhero. It's Marv!'

Joe pushed his way to the front of the crowd, a wide grin on his face.

'Don't worry everyone, Marv will save the day just like always and we'll be back inside Wave World before you know it!' Joe shouted. A few people in a crowd even cheered. Grandad gave him two thumbs up. Marv's cheeks felt hot. It was nice to hear all the cheers and Joe's confidence in him. But what if they were all wrong? Marv knew that to stop Hydro and her sharks he'd have to go into the water. What if even the super-suit couldn't help Marv overcome his fear?

CHAPTER 4

Marv gulped and walked into the water park. The giant inflatable castle floated in the biggest pool, with the sharks patrolling the water around it. Hydro pranced around on top of the castle. She didn't even look in Marv's direction, it was like he didn't even exist.

ENTRANCE

'Hey, Hydro!' Marv called as he walked towards the pool. 'I'm Marv, the superhero.' Hydro kept on ignoring him. 'I said that my name is Marv!'

'I heard you the first time,' Hydro replied.

'Okay, but why didn't you answer?'

'Because I don't listen to losers!'

'SUPERVILLAIN DETECTED!

SUPERVILLAIN DETECTED!

SUPERVILLAIN DETECTED!'

Pixel cried out in between beeps.

'Haven't you already done that? I thought she was already detected.' Marv said.

'I apologize, it appears that she was giving off such high supervillain vibes that it triggered my supervillain alarm twice,' Pixel replied nervously.

'That's fair,' Marv said before turning back to Hydro. 'Why can't you just send your sharks away. The water park is big enough for everyone, so why can't you just share?'

58

'Share?!' Hydro threw her head back
and laughed at the top of her lungs. 'Why
would I share when I can just have it all?!'

'Because it's the right thing to do,'
Marv said.

'No! This water park is now part of my kingdom,' Hydro cried. 'I have a castle, and I'm the ruler so everyone has to do what I say!'

The castle was floating away from Marv towards the centre of the pool. It was much too far for him to jump to, and he didn't want to swim. There was only one way he could get there and stop Hydro. Marv pressed the M on his suit.

IT'S SUPER-SUIT TIME!' Marv said. 'Super suit, please activate flying mode!'

The suit rumbled and then a pair of rockets popped out of the side of Marv's boots, and a big jet pack pushed out of the suit's back. Marv whooshed up into the air as his jet pack blasted into

action. Pixel whizzed alongside him. Marv felt a big grin spread across his face. Maybe he could defeat this villain without getting in the water at all?

'My fear—I mean
my robot calculations
that something might
go wrong has gone up
1000%,' Pixel blurted out.

'We'll be fine, Pixel,' Marv said.

'Are you sure?' Pixel pointed at the castle.

Huge inflatable cannons sat at the top of the castle, and they were pointing straight at the dynamic duo. Hydro ran from cannon to cannon in a blur. She moved so fast that it looked as though she was controlling all of them at the same time.

'Okay, maybe we won't be fine. We need to dodge!'

Marv and Pixel split up, flying in opposite directions.

A huge **BOOM** came from one of the cannons. As quick as a flash, a huge ball of water flew past them, just missing.

BoOM!

BoOM!

BoOM!

Marv whizzed to the left and dodged
one blast of water. Then he whizzed to
the right and dodged another. Just as he

was about to dodge a third one he looked down. Marv was flying right above the big pool. It was so big that the water seemed to be endless.

THE PANIC gripped him tight. Marv couldn't move! Then **SPLASH**, the water cannon hit Marv, completely drenching him.

Marv's jet pack spluttered and burped out thick smoke. It wasn't working properly anymore!

'ARGH!' Marv yelled as he fell through the air. Wind whooshed past his face and his stomach backflipped. He was about to plunge into the shark-infested water. He closed his eyes and waited for the splash. Then came a

splutter and roar as the
jetpack burst back to life.
Quickly, Marv turned his
body, swerving away
from the pool and
crashing into a huge
pile of inflatables.

'Are you okay?' Pixel rushed over to him, helping Marv to his feet. The jetpack disappeared back into his suit.

'Yes.' Marv said but then he hung his head. **THE PANIC**. 'Actually, no, I'm sorry but I'm too scared of the water. I can't defeat Hydro.'

'Of course you can,' Pixel replied. 'I believe in you, Marv.'

Marv sighed for a moment then stopped—he could hear something. Voices! He spun around on his heels. Everyone who had been chased out by Hydro and her sharks stood at the entrance to the Water Park, and they were all cheering his name.

The more they went on the louder they got.

Marv spotted Grandad in the crowd. He was moving in a weird way, his arms were together above his head and he kept bending his knees. It was almost like he was diving. *Sometimes you just have to jump.* Marv heard his grandad's voice in his head. Marv knew he had to stop Hydro, and he couldn't let fear stand in his way.

As Marv slowly walked towards the edge of the pool again, he could feel **THE PANIC** rising through his body—it felt like ants crawling on his skin.

Marv reached over to the 'M' on his chest and pressed his hand onto it.

'Suit, pleeeease help me swim,' Marv said. He waited for a moment, but nothing happened. His suit was exactly the same. Maybe it had stopped working? 'Suit, pretty please help me swim,' Marv said again, but still, nothing changed.

'Just believe in yourself, Marv, and the suit will do the rest,' Pixel chirped. Was it really that easy? 'The suit can help you, but you have to believe,' Pixel finished.

Marv didn't know what would happen, but he had to try. So, Marv closed his eyes tight. **THE PANIC** didn't go but slowly, Marv began to feel another, stronger feeling—**COURAGE!**

Marv leapt forward into the pool with a great splash. He kicked his legs and thrust his arms back and forth, just like he had been taught in his swimming lessons. With each movement of his arms and legs, his suit changed. His gloves became webbed and his feet turned into flippers.

Marv surged through the water, moving through it faster than he had ever done before. He was gliding so smoothly through the cool water. It felt **AMAZING!** His arms and legs pulled him along the surface of the water with such ease that he didn't even have to think about staying afloat. He could swim!

With this much confidence, no amount of **THE PANIC** would get him out of the water.

Now he could reach the fortress and take on Hydro, but first, he'd have to deal with the sharks! Marv just needed a little bit of help to do it. One of Hydro's doughnut inflatables was in the water— it was just what he needed! Marv took

a huge breath and then dived down
through the water and towards
the sharks.

Now that Marv
could see them up
close he noticed
that instead of
their fins being
white or blue
they were a
weird silvery
colour.

The colour of the sharks reminded Marv of Pixel . . . He got it now, they were robots!

All three robot sharks swivelled around to stare at Marv and his heart leapt in his chest. It was time to get going. He swam away and the sharks swooshed through the water after him. Marv was swimming as fast as he could, but they were faster. They quickly caught up and began to snap at his heels. The sharks bumped heads, pushing each other out of the way, as they tried to be the first to get a bite of Marv.

Marv swam to the left, and then the right, just about escaping the sharks' teeth. Then without warning, Marv suddenly swam up towards the surface. The sharks were right on his tail. Marv burst out of the water, through the hole of the doughnut inflatable and landed on the side of the pool. The sharks tried to follow him, pushing through the doughnut hole, all at once. But they were too big.

The three robot sharks lay helpless, trapped in the inflatable, squished against each other, chomping on thin air.

Pixel beeped and clapped.

'Could all sharks wearing a doughnut inflatable, please leave the pool—your time is up!' Marv said to the stuck sharks.

They just snarled at him.

'SUPERVILLAIN DETECTED!

SUPERVILLAIN DETECTED!

SUPERVILLAIN DETECTED!'

Pixel said for the third time that day,
pointing at Hydro at the top of the
inflatable castle. Marv raised his
eyebrows. 'Sorry, I really do need to get
that checked.'

'No worries Pixel,' Marv said, rubbing
the top of Pixel's head. 'Let's go!'

CHAPTER 5

Marv jumped into the air, his jetpacks were back out and firing on all cylinders. He flew back up towards the inflatable castle.

Hydro leapt over to her cannons once more and began to fire.

BANG! BANG! BANG! BANG!

The balls of water rushed towards Marv so quickly that he barely had time to think. This time **THE PANIC** wouldn't stop him. Marv twirled to the left and then the right, smoothly swooping out of the way of them. It felt as though he was swimming through the air. Those water bombs had no chance to hit him now! Hydro stomped her feet in frustration.

Marv's heart was pounding with excitement, but his mind was clear, he knew exactly what he had to do.

He soared closer to the Castle. 'Super-suit, please activate deflating dart!' A dart gun rose out from Marv's wrist and fired a dart straight into the wall of the inflatable castle.

POP!

The castle began to spin
wildly as it deflated, sinking
into the water.

'You may have stopped my robot sharks, but a loser like you could never catch me!' Hydro yelled, diving from the castle and into the pool below.

In a blink of an eye Hydro was up, out of the water, and sprinting away. Marv went after her.

It was hard for Marv to keep track of Hydro. She was running so fast that it looked like she was disappearing and reappearing.

That must have been
her superpower!

Marv did his best to keep up. She led them to the rapids. Rushing water swept and splashed over rocks, it was moving so fast!

Hydro jumped into an inflatable dinghy on the water and began to row. Marv and Pixel jumped into the boat behind hers. 'Woah!' Marv cried. Even before they started moving, the dinghy was wobbling all over the place. Marv and Pixel began to row as hard as they could. It was a bumpy ride. The water felt alive here and it pushed and pulled them in all directions.

Hydro had a headstart, but she couldn't beat Marv and Pixel's teamwork.

'Just give up!' Marv yelled over the sound of the rushing water.

Hydro shook her head and cackled.

'No way! You're gonna have to do better than that,' she said, and her dinghy surged forward just out of reach of Marv and Pixel.

Whenever Marv and Pixel would get closer to Hydro, she managed to pull ahead of them. Until eventually, just when it looked like they'd caught up with her for good, Hydro leapt from her dinghy.

Marv and Pixel were quick to follow and were only a couple of steps behind her. Hydro looked tired out now. She was huffing and puffing. Marv was sure that they were just about to catch up when Hydro dashed towards the entrance to a ride. It wasn't until he'd chased Hydro to the top of the steep flight of stairs that Marv realized where he was—this was the Doom Flume, the tall water slide that spiralled high up above the park. It so high up that it made Marv's knees knock. More worrying than that was the fact that Hydro had completely vanished. Marv was sure that she had come up here, so where was she now?

'Looking for me?' came a voice from behind Marv. He spun around to see Hydro waiting behind him. 'Bet you didn't see this coming!' Hydro shoved Marv and Pixel onto the slide.

THE PANIC started to rise again, but Marv couldn't give in to his fear. Before the water could carry him and Pixel down, he turned, and a rope shot out of the arm of his suit, wrapping itself around Hydro's foot. As Marv fell down the slide he dragged Hydro with him.

All three of them swooshed down the water slide. They held on tight to each other. Heroes, villains, and sidekicks are, of course, all scared of giant slides. They screamed as it rocketed them up, then down, left, then right, before dumping them into a pool with a great, big **SPLASH**.

Marv swam over to the edge of the pool and lifted Pixel out. He stayed in the water. **THE PANIC** was something small now. He liked the water.

Hydro scurried out of the pool looking bedraggled.

'Curse you, Marv! You think you're all cool now because you can swim really well and saved Wave World and have a cool costume and have an awesome robot sidekick!' she yelled.

'Yes. I think he's cool,' said Pixel, hovering over Hydro.

'Well, you're wrong!' Hydro grabbed the giant doughnut inflatable with the sad robot sharks in it and disappeared once and for all.

CHAPTER 6

Everyone flooded back into Wave World. People couldn't wait to get back to having fun. Marv got out of the pool and watched for a moment with a smile on his face, then he felt a tug at the leg of his suit. It was Pixel. She gave him a nod, then he scooped her up and ran back outside.

When they were far away from everyone else Marv put Pixel down.

'I detected that your heart rate was faster than normal, especially while you were swimming. Were you scared?' Pixel asked.

Marv bit his lip and hesitated.

'Yes, I was.'

'Ah, so was I! I'm scared all the time.' Pixel said with a bright smile.

'But you're a robot, you can't be scared!'

'Why not?' Pixel said. 'Everyone gets scared sometimes. Even me.'

'High-five for being scared,' Marv grinned. He didn't feel alone anymore.

'High-five!' Pixel replied.

Marv changed out of his super-suit, Pixel hopped into his swimming bag and they went back towards the main pool.

Marv was back to being Marvin.

Marvin's grandad walked over to him and wrapped him up in a big hug.

'Good job back there,' Grandad whispered. He pulled his sunglasses down and gave Marv a wink. 'Now go find your friend, I'm sure you have a lot of lost time to make up for.'

Joe ran up to Marvin and threw an arm over his shoulder.

'Another day saved by Marv! You missed it again though. It's weird, it's like you're never around when Marv is. I wonder why that is?' Joe said.

'I—I guess it's just a coincidence.' Did Joe know his secret? Marvin couldn't tell.

'Yeah, I'm sure it is.' Joe grinned.

Marvin paused.

'I'm sorry about before. When I kept avoiding getting in the pool. It's just . . . I'm scared of water,' he blurted out.

'Wait, what?' Joe's jaw dropped. 'You're scared of water!? But you were a great swimmer in all our lessons.'

'The lessons feel different to swimming by myself!' Marvin replied.

Joe dropped his head.

'I'm sorry. I wouldn't have asked you to go to a water park if I knew you were scared,' Joe said.

'I know. I should have told you.' Marvin's head dropped too.

Joe stopped and pointed towards the exit.

'Do you want to leave? We shouldn't stay here if you're scared,' Joe said.

'No, I want to be here, even if I get a bit scared.' Marvin smiled and Joe smiled back at him. He was so glad he had Joe as a best friend. 'I'm glad you invited me too,' Marvin said.

'Good. And who knows, maybe being around water all day has helped you overcome some of your fears,' Joe said, walking towards the big pool again.

'Maybe.' Marvin hesitated. He felt that antsy feeling in his chest again. **THE PANIC**. What if his suit was the only

reason that he could have fun in the pool? What if without his suit the water park would be too scary for him?

Marvin took a really deep breath and remembered the truth.
His suit hadn't made him feel any less scared in the pool. Marvin had to believe, he had to find his courage before the super-suit would even work. That's what helped him overcome **THE PANIC**.

Marvin joined Joe in the big pool.
They splashed around and had a great
time.

'What do you think about the big water slide over there? We could ride it!' Marvin pointed at the Doom Flume.

'That looks really big. Are you sure we'll be okay?' Joe suddenly looked very pale.

'It does look little bit scary, but I bet it's fun.' Marvin grinned. 'All we need is a bit of courage.'

'Okay, let's try it.' Joe grinned back.

So, they got out of the pool and walked off to the water slide, together.

ABOUT THE AUTHOR

ALEX FALASE-KOYA

Alex is a London native. He has been writing children's fiction since he was a teenager and was a winner of Spread the Word's 2019 London Writers Awards for YA and Children's. He co-wrote The Breakfast Club Adventures is the first fiction book by Marcus Rashford. He now lives in Walthamstow with his girlfriend and two cats.

ABOUT THE ILLUSTRATOR

PAULA BOWLES

Paula grew up in Hertfordshire, and has
always loved drawing, reading, and using
her imagination, so she studied illustration
at Falmouth College of Arts and became an
illustrator. She now lives in Bristol, and has
worked as an illustrator for over ten years, and
has had books published with Nosy Crow and
Simon & Schuster.

MARV

Marvin's life changed when he found an old superhero suit and became MARV. The suit has been passed down through Marvin's family and was last worn by his grandad. It's powered by the kindness and imagination of the wearer and doesn't work for just anybody.

COURAGE	7
FRIENDSHIP	9
KINDNESS	9
POWERS	10
AGILITY	7
COMBAT SKILLS	6

PIXEL

PIXEL is Marv's brave superhero sidekick. Her quick thinking and unwavering loyalty make her the perfect crime-fighting companion.

COURAGE	6
FRIENDSHIP	10
KINDNESS	9
POWERS	5
AGILITY	7
COMBAT SKILLS	5

HYDRO

HYDRO is a villain with superspeed. She moves so quickly that, to anyone watching, she seems like a blur, or like she's disappeared completely! Hydro loves water because her powers are at their strongest when she's close to it..

COURAGE	6
FRIENDSHIP	3
KINDNESS	3
POWERS	8
AGILITY	7
COMBAT SKILLS	7

'THE SUPER-SUIT IS POWERED BY TWO THINGS: **KINDNESS** AND **IMAGINATION**. LUCKILY YOU, MARVIN, HAVE TONS OF BOTH!'

SUIT UP. STEP UP.
IT'S TIME TO BECOME A HERO!

MARV

AND THE
DINO
ATTACK

WRITTEN BY
ALEX FALASE-KOYA

PICTURES BY
PAULA BOWLES

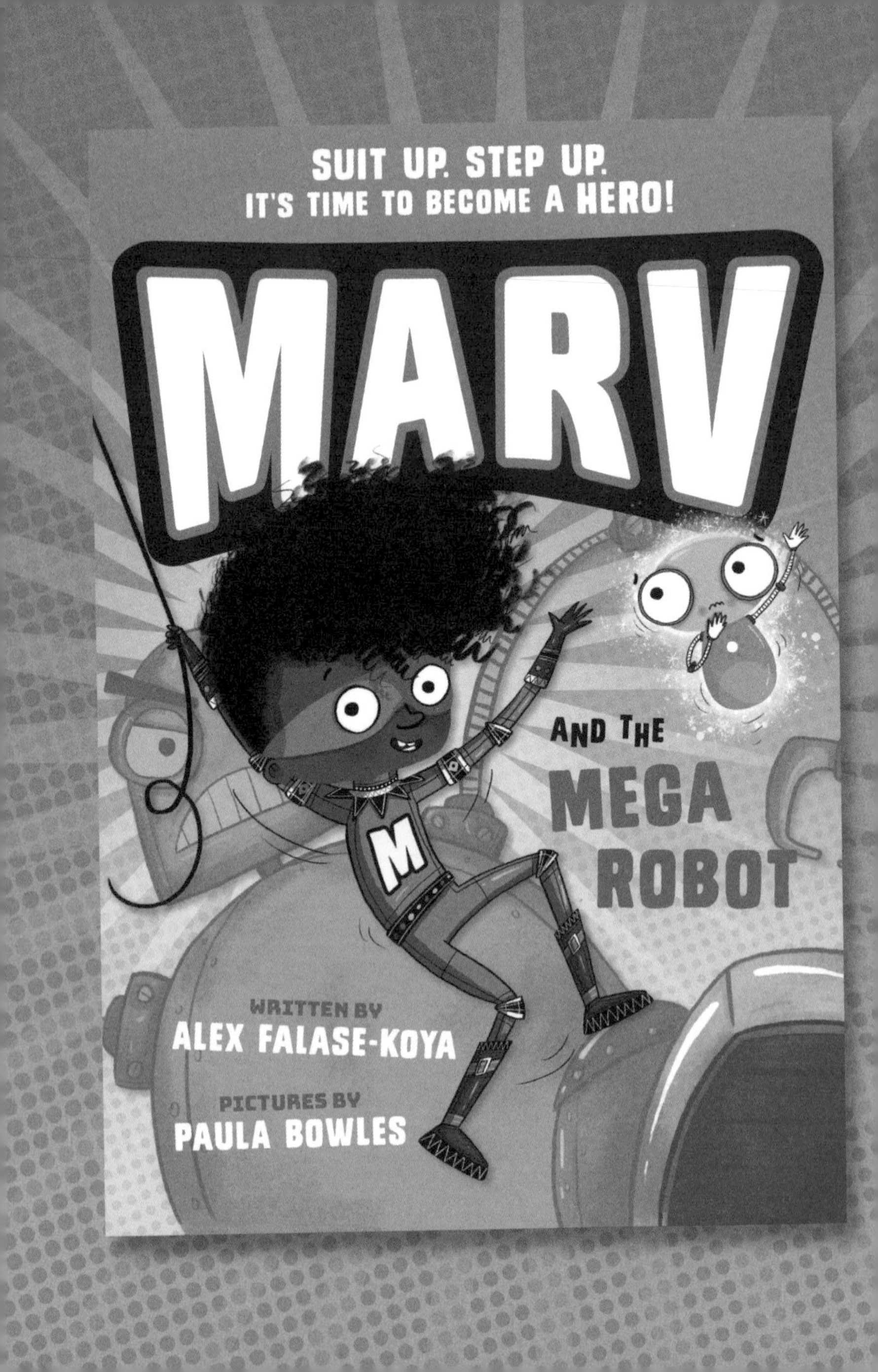
SUIT UP. STEP UP.
IT'S TIME TO BECOME A HERO!
MARV
AND THE
MEGA
ROBOT
WRITTEN BY
ALEX FALASE-KOYA
PICTURES BY
PAULA BOWLES

**'THE SUPER-SUIT IS POWERED BY TWO THINGS:
KINDNESS AND IMAGINATION.
LUCKILY YOU, MARVIN, HAVE TONS OF BOTH!'**

Marvin loves reading about superheroes and now he's about to become one for real.

Grandad is passing his superhero suit and robot sidekick, Pixel, on to Marvin. It's been a long time since the world needed a superhero but now, with a mega robot and a supervillain on the loose, that time has come.

To defeat his enemies and protect his friends, Marvin must learn to trust the superhero within. Only then will Marvin become MARV – unstoppable, invincible, and **totally marvellous!**

LOVE MARV?
WHY NOT TRY THESE TOO...?